IN LETTERS OF FIRE

BY

GASTON LEROUX

British Library Cataloguing-in-Publication Data
A catalogue record for this book is available from the
British Library

CONTENTS

GASTON LEROUX

Gaston Louis Alfred Leroux was born in Paris in 1868. In his youth he enjoyed sailing and fishing, and attended school in Caen, where he began writing poetry and short stories while studying the works of Victor Hugo and Alexandre Dumas. He then travelled to Paris to study law, obtaining his degree in 1889 despite the fact that he had largely lost interest in the profession. When his father died in that same year, Leroux inherited a large amount of money, and lived wildly for a while, developing a taste for expensive food and wine and high-stakes gambling. In 1890 he started working as a court reporter and theatre critic for *L'Écho de Paris*, and then went on to become international correspondent for the Parisian newspaper *Le Matin*.

As a noted reporter, Leroux attended trials, interviewed prisoners, and observed executions by guillotine. He also travelled widely, finding himself in Russia during the 1905 revolution, and even getting as far as Asia and Africa, witnessing first-hand some remarkable events of his time. Leroux began to dabble in fiction, producing *Seeking of the Morning's Treasures* in 1903, and four years later he abandoned journalism altogether to focus on his fiction. In 1908 he published *The Mystery of the Yellow Room*, starring the amateur detective Joseph Rouletabille. Rouletabille went on to feature in a number of popular novels, and Leroux's contribution to French detective fiction is now viewed as parallel to Sir Arthur Conan Doyle's in the United Kingdom. Aside from his detective fiction, Leroux is best-remembered in the English-speaking world for his 1910 novel *The Phantom of the Opera*, which has spawned a number of well-known adaptations.

Leroux died in Nice, France in 1927, having published almost fifty novels.

IN LETTERS OF FIRE

Gaston Leroux

We had been out hunting wild boars all day, when we were overtaken by a violent storm, which compelled us to seek refuge in a deep cavern. It was Makoko, our guide, who took upon himself to give utterance to the thought which haunted the minds of the four of us who had sought safety from the fury of the tempest – Mathis, Allan, Makoko, and myself.

"If the gentleman who lives in yonder house, which is said to be haunted by the devil, does not grant us the shelter of his roof tonight, we shall be compelled to sleep here."

Hardly had he uttered the words when a strange figure appeared at the entrance to the cavern.

"It is *he*!" exclaimed Makoko, grasping my arm.

I stared at the stranger.

He was tall, lanky, of bony frame, and melancholy aspect. Unconscious of our presence, he stood leaning on his fowling-piece at the entrance of the cavern, showing a strong aquiline nose, a thin moustache, a stern mouth, and lack-lustre eyes. He was bareheaded; his hair was thin, while a few grey locks fell behind his ears. His age might have been anywhere between forty and sixty. He must have been strikingly handsome in the days when the light still shone in those time-dimmed eyes and those bitter lips could still break into a smile – but handsome in a haughty and forbidding style. A kind of terrible energy still lurked beneath his features, spectral as those of an apparition.

By his side stood a hairless dog, low on its legs, which was evidently barking at us. Yet we could hear nothing! The dog, it was plain, was dumb, and *barked at us in silence*!

Suddenly the man turned towards us, and said in a voice of the most exquisite politeness:

"Gentlemen, it is out of the question for you to return to La Chaux-de-Fonds tonight. Permit me to offer you my hospitality."

Then, bending over his dog, he said:

"Stop barking, Mystère."

The dog closed his jaws at once.

Makoko emitted a grunt. During the five hours that we had been enjoying the chase, Mathis and Makoko had told Allan and myself, who were strangers to the district, some strange and startling stories about our host, whom they represented as having had, like Faust, dealings with the Evil Spirit.

It was not without some trepidation, therefore, that we all moved out of the cavern.

"Gentlemen," said the stranger, with a melancholy smile, "it is many a long year since my door was thrown open to visitors. I am not fond of society, but I must tell you that one night, six months ago, a youth who had lost his way came and knocked at that door and begged for shelter till the morning. I refused him his request. Next day a body was found at the bottom of the big marl-pit – a body partly devoured by wolves."

"Why, that must have been Petit-Leduc!" cried Makoko. "So you were heartless enough to turn the poor lad away, at night and in the midst of winter! You are his murderer!"

"Truly spoken," replied the man, simply. "It was I who killed him. And now you see, gentlemen, that the incident has rendered me hospitable."

"Would you tell us why you drove him from your door?" growled Makoko.

"Because," he replied, quietly, "my house brings

misfortune."

"I would rather risk meeting the powers of darkness than catching a cold in the head," I retorted, laughing, and without further parley we set off, and in a short while had reached the door of the ancient mansion, which stood among the most desolate surroundings, on a shelf of barren rock, swept by all the winds of heaven.

The huge door, antique, iron-barred, and studded with enormous nails, revolved slowly on its hinges, and opened noiselessly. A shrunken little old dame was there to welcome us.

From the threshold we could see a large, high room, somewhat similar to the room formerly styled the retainers' hall. It certainly constituted a part of what remained of the castle, on the ruins of which the mansion had been erected some centuries before. It was fully lighted by the fire on the enormous hearth, where a huge log was burning, and by two petrol lamps hanging by chains from the stone roof. There was no furniture except a heavy table of white wood, a large armchair upholstered in leather, a few stools, and a rude sideboard.

We walked the length of the room. The old woman opened a door. We found ourselves at the foot of a worm-eaten staircase with sunken steps. This staircase, a spiral one, led to the second storey of the building, where the old woman showed us to our rooms.

To this day I can recall our host – were I to live a hundred years I could not forget that figure such as it appeared to me, as if framed by the fireplace – when I went into the hall where Mother Appenzel had spread our supper.

He was standing in front of my friends, on the stone hearth of that enormous fireplace. He was in evening dress – but such evening dress! It was in the pink of fashion, but a fashion long since vanished. The high collar of the coat, the broad lapels, the velvet waistcoat, the silken knee-breeches and stockings, the cravat, all seemed to possess the elegance of days gone by.

By his side lay his dog Mystère, his massive jaws parted in a yawn – yawning, just as he had barked, *in silence.*

"Has your dog been dumb for long?" I ventured to ask. "What strange accident has happened to him?"

"He has been dumb from his birth," replied my host, after a slight pause, as if this topic of conversation did not please him.

Still, I persisted in my questions.

"Was his father dumb – or perhaps his mother?"

"His mother, and his mother's mother," he replied, still coldly, "and *her* mother also."

"So you were the master of Mystère's great-grandmother?"

"I was, sir. She was indeed a faithful creature, and one who loved me well. A marvellous watch-dog," added my host, displaying sudden signs of emotion which surprised me.

"And she also was dumb from her birth?"

"No, sir. No, she was not born dumb – *but she became so one night when she had barked too much!*"

There was a world of meaning in the tone with which he spoke these words that at the moment I did not understand.

Supper was served. During the meal the conversation did not languish. Our host inquired whether we liked our rooms.

"I have a favour to beg of you," I ventured to say. "I should like to sleep in the haunted room!"

No sooner had I uttered the sentence than our host's pale face became still paler.

"Who has told you that there was a haunted room in this house?" he asked, striving with difficulty to restrain an evident irritation.

Mother Appenzel, who had just entered, trembled violently.

"It was you, Mother Appenzel?"

"Pray do not scold the good woman," I said; "my indiscreet behaviour alone must bear the blame. I was attempting to enter a room, the door of which was closed, when your servant forbade me to do so. 'Do not go into the haunted chamber,' she said."

"And you naturally did not do so?"

"Well, yes; I did go in."

"Heaven protect us!" wailed Mother Appenzel, letting fall a tumbler, which broke into pieces.

"Begone!" cried her master. Then, turning to us, he added, "You are indeed full of curiosity, gentlemen!"

"Pray pardon us if we are so," I said. "Moreover, permit me to remind you that it was you yourself who alluded to the rumours current on the mountainside. Well, it would afford me much pleasure if your generous hospitality should be the occasion of dispersing them. When I have slept in the room which enjoys so evil a reputation, and have rested there peacefully, it will no longer be said that, to use your own expression, '*your* house brings misfortune.'"

Our host interrupted me: "You shall not sleep in that room; it is no longer used as a bedroom. No one has slept there for fifty years past."

"Who, then, was the last one to sleep in it?"

"I myself – and I should not advise anyone to sleep in it after me!"

"Fifty years ago, you say! You could only be a child at the time, at an age when one is still afraid at nights—"

"Fifty years ago I was twenty-eight!"

"Am I committing an indiscretion when asking you what happened to you in that room? I have just come from visiting it, and nothing whatever happened to me. The room seems to me the most natural of rooms. I even attempted to prop up a wardrobe which seemed as if it were about to fall forward on its face."

"You laid hands on the wardrobe!" cried the man, throwing down his table-napkin, and coming towards me with the gleam of madness in his eyes. "You actually laid hands on the wardrobe?"

"Yes," was my quiet answer; "as I say, it seemed about to fall."

"But it cannot fall! It will never fall! Never again will it stand upright! It is its nature to be in that position for all time to come, trembling with fear for all eternity!"

We had all risen. The man's voice was harsh as he spoke these most mysterious words. Heavy drops of perspiration trickled down his face. Those eyes of his, which we had thought dimmed for ever, flashed with fury. He was indeed awful to contemplate. He grasped my wrist and wrung it with a strength of which I would have deemed him incapable.

"You did not open it?"

"No."

"Then you do not know what is in it? No? Well, all the better! By Heaven, I tell you, sir, it is all the better for *you*!".

Turning towards his dog, he shouted:

"To your kennel! When will you find your voice again, Mystère? Or are you going to die like the others – *in silence?*"

He had opened the door leading to a tower, and went out, driving the dog before him.

We were deeply moved at this unexpected scene. The man had disappeared in the darkness of the tower, still pursuing his dog.

"What did I tell you?" remarked Makoko, in a scarcely audible tone. "You may all please yourselves, but, as for me, I do not intend to sleep here tonight. I shall sit up here in this hall until daybreak."

"And so shall I," added Mathis.

Makoko, bending over us, his eyes staring out of their sockets, continued: "Do you not see that he is a madman?"

"You two fellows with your death-mask faces," exclaimed Allan, "are not going to prevent us from enjoying ourselves. Supposing we start a game of écarté. We will ask our host to take a hand; it will divert his thoughts."

An extraordinary fellow was Allan. His fondness for card-playing amounted to a mania. He pulled out a pack of cards, and had hardly done so when our host re-entered the hall. He was now comparatively calm, but no sooner had he perceived the pack of cards on the table than his features became transformed, and assumed such an expression of fear and fury that I myself was terrified.

"Cards!" he cried. "You have cards!"

Allan rose and said, pleasantly:

"We have decided not to retire for the night. We are about to have a friendly little game of écarté. Do you know the game?"

Allan stopped. He also had been struck with the fearful expression on our host's face. His eyes were bloodshot, the sparse hairs of his moustache stood out bristling, his teeth gleamed, while his lips hissed out the words:

"Cards! Cards!"

The words escaped with difficulty from his throat, as if some invisible hand were clutching it.

"Who sent you here with cards? What do you want with me? The cards must be burnt – they must be burnt!"

Of a sudden he grasped the pack and was about to cast it into the flames, but he stopped just on the point of doing so, his trembling fingers let drop the cards, and he sank into the armchair, exclaiming hoarsely:

"I am suffocating; I am suffocating!"

We rushed to his succour, but with a single effort of his bony fingers he had already torn off his collar and his cravat; and now, motionless, holding his head erect, and settling down in the huge armchair, he burst into tears.

"You are good fellows," he said at last, in milder tones. "You shall know everything. You shall not leave this house in ignorance, taking me for a madman – for a poor, miserable, melancholy madman.

"Yes, indeed," he continued; "yes, you shall know everything. It may be of use to you."

He rose, paced up and down, then halted in front of us, staring at us with the dimmed look that had given way to the momentary flash.

"Sixty years ago I was entering upon my eighteenth year. With all the overweening presumption of youth, I was sceptical of everything. Nature had fashioned me strong and handsome. Fate had endowed me with enormous wealth. I became the most fashionable youth of my day. Paris, gentlemen, with all its pleasures, was for ten years at my feet. When I had reached the age of twenty-eight I was on the brink of ruin. There remained to me between two and three hundred thousand francs and this manor, with the land surrounding it.

"Just at that time, gentlemen, I fell madly in love with an angelic creature. I could never have dreamt of the existence of such beauty and purity. The girl whom I adored was ignorant of the passionate love which was consuming me, and she remained so. Her family was one of the wealthiest in all Europe. For nothing in this world would I have had her suspect that I aspired to the honour of her hand in order to replenish my empty coffers with her dowry. So I went the way of the gambling-dens, in the vain hope of recovering my vanished millions. I lost all, and one fine evening I left Paris to come and bury myself in this old mansion, my sole refuge.

"I found here an old man, Father Appenzel; his granddaughter, of whom later on I made a servant; and his grandson, a child of tender years, who grew up to manhood on the estate, and who is now my steward. I fell prey, on the very evening of my arrival, to despair and ennui. The astounding events that followed took place that very evening.

"When I went up to my room – the room which one of you has asked to be allowed to occupy tonight – I had made up my mind to take my own life. A brace of pistols lay on the chest of drawers. Suddenly, as I was putting my hand on one of the pistols, my dog began to howl in the courtyard – to howl as I have never heard the wind howl, unless it be tonight.

" 'So,' thought I, 'here is Mystère raising a death-howl. She must know that I am going to kill myself tonight.'

"I toyed with the pistol, recalling of a sudden what my past life had been, and wondering for the first time what my death would be like. Suddenly my eye lighted on the titles of a few old books which stood on a shelf hanging above the chest of drawers. I was surprised to see that all of them dealt with sorcerers and matters appertaining to the powers of evil. I took up a book, *The Sorcerers of the Jura*, and, with the sceptical smile of the man who has defied Fate, I opened it. The first two lines, printed in red, at once caught my eye:

" *'He who seriously wishes to see the devil has but to summon him with his whole heart, and he will come.'*

"Then followed the story of an individual who, like myself, a lover in despair – like myself, a ruined man – had in all sincerity summoned to his help the Prince of Darkness, and who had been assisted by him; for, a few months later, he had once more become incredibly rich and had married his beloved. I read the story to the end.

" 'Well, here was a lucky fellow!' I exclaimed, tossing the book on to the chest of drawers. Mystère was still howling in the grounds. I parted the window-curtains, and could not help shuddering when I saw the dog's shadow dancing in the moonlight. It really seemed as if the slut was possessed of some evil spirit, for her movements were inexplicably eccentric. She seemed to be snapping at some invisible form!

"I tried to laugh over the matter, but the state of my mind, the story I had just read, the howling of the dog, her strange leaps, the sinister locality, the old room, the pistols which I myself had loaded, all had contributed to take a greater hold of my imagination than I dared confess.

"Leaving the window I strolled about the room for awhile. Of a sudden I saw myself in the mirror of the wardrobe. My pallor was such that I thought that I was dead. Alas, no! The man standing before the wardrobe was not dead. It was, on the contrary, a living man who, with all his heart, was summoning the King of Lost Souls.

"Yes, with all my heart. I was too young to die; I wished to enjoy life for a while yet; to be rich once more; for her, for her sake, for the one who was an angel. Yes, yes, I, I myself summoned the devil!

"And then, in the mirror, side by side with my form, something appeared – something superhuman – a pale object – a mist, a terrible little cloud which was soon transformed into eyes – eyes of fearful loveliness. Another form was standing resplendent beside my haggard face; a mouth – a mouth which said to me, 'Open!' At this I recoiled. But the mouth was still saying to me, 'Open, open, if you dare!'

"Then something knocked three times upon the door inside the wardrobe – and the door flew open of its own accord!"

Just at that instant the old man's narrative was interrupted by three knocks on the door, which suddenly opened, and a man entered.

"Was it you who knocked like that, Guillaume?" asked our host, striving in vain to regain his composure.

"Yes, master."

"I had given you up for tonight. You saw the notary?"

"Yes; and I did not care to keep so great a sum of money about my person."

We gathered that Guillaume was the gentleman's steward. He advanced to the table, took a little bag from the folds of his cloak, extracted some documents from it, and laid them on the table. Then he drew an envelope from his bag, emptied its contents on the table, and counted out twelve one-thousand-franc notes.

"There's the purchase-money for Misery Wood."

"Good, Guillaume," said our host, picking up the banknotes and replacing them in the envelope. "You must be hungry. Are you going to sleep here tonight?"

"No; it is impossible. I have to call on the farmer. We have some business to transact together early in the morning. However, I do not mind having a bit of supper."

"Go to Mother Appenzel, my good fellow; she will take good care of you," adding, as the steward strode towards the kitchen, "Take away all those rubbishy papers."

The man picked up the documents, while the gentleman, taking a pocket-book out of his pocket, placed the envelope containing the twelve notes into it and returned the book to his pocket.

Then, resuming his narrative, in reply to a request from Makoko, he continued:

"You wish to know what the wardrobe contained? Well, I am going to tell you. There was something which I saw – something which scorched my eyes. There shone within the recess of the wardrobe, written in letters of fire, three words:

" 'THOU SHALT WIN!'

"Yes," he continued, in a gloomy tone, "the devil had, in three words, expressed, in characters of fire, in the depths of the wardrobe, the fate that awaited me. He had left behind him his sign-manual, the irrefutable proof of the hideous pact into which I had entered with him on that tragic night. 'Thou shalt win!' A ruined gamester, I sought to become rich, and he told me: 'Thou shalt win!' In three short words he granted me the world's wealth. 'Thou shalt win!'

"Next morning old Appenzel found me lying unconscious at the foot of the wardrobe. Alas! when I had recovered my senses I had forgotten nothing. I was fated never to forget what I had seen. Wherever I go, wherever I wend my steps, be it night, be it day, I read the fiery phrase, 'Thou shalt win!'

– on the walls of darkness, on the resplendent orb of the sun, on the earth and in the skies, within myself when I close my eyes, on your faces when I look at you!"

The old man, exhausted, ceased speaking, and fell back, moaning, into the armchair.

"I must tell you," he resumed, after a few moments, "that my experience had had so terrifying an effect on me that I had been compelled to stay in bed, where Father Appenzel brought me a soothing potion of herbs. Addressing me, he said: 'Something incredible has happened, sir. Your dog has become dumb. *She barks in silence!*'

" 'Oh, I know, I understand!' I exclaimed. 'She will not recover her voice until *he* shall have returned!'

"Father Appenzel looked at me in amazement and fright, for my hair was standing on end. In spite of myself, my gaze was straying towards the wardrobe. Father Appenzel, as alarmed and agitated as myself, went on to say:

" 'When I found you, sir, on the floor this morning the wardrobe was inclined as it is now, while its door was open. I closed it, but I was unable to get it to stand upright. It seems always on the point of falling forward.'

"I begged old Appenzel to leave me to myself. I got out of bed, went to the wardrobe and opened its door. Conceive, I pray you, my feelings when I had done so. The sentence, that sentence written in characters of fire, was still there! It was graven in the boards at the back; it had burnt the boards with its imprint; and by day I read what I had read by night – the words: 'Thou shalt win.'

"I flew out of the room. I called for help. Father Appenzel returned. I said to him: 'Look into the depths of that wardrobe, and tell me what you see there!'

"My servant did as I bid him, and said to me: 'Thou shalt win!'

"I dressed myself. I fled like a madman from the accursed house, and wandered in the mountains. The mountain air did me good. When I came home in the evening I was perfectly calm; I had thought matters over; my dog might have become dumb through some perfectly natural physiological phenomenon. With regard to the sentence in the wardrobe, it had not come there of itself, and, as I had not had any previous acquaintance with that piece of furniture, it was probable that the three fatal words had been there for countless years, inscribed by someone addicted to the black art, following upon some gambling affair which was no concern of mine.

"I ate my supper, and went to bed in the same room. The night passed without incident.

"Next day I went to La Chaux-de-Fonds, to call on a notary. All that this adventure with the wardrobe had succeeded in doing was to imbue me with the idea of tempting fate in the shape of cards, one last time, ere putting into execution my idea about suicide. I borrowed a few one-thousand-franc notes on the security of the estate, and I took train for Paris. As I ascended the staircase of the club I recalled my nightmare, and remarked to myself ironically, for I placed no faith in the success of this supreme attempt: 'We shall now see whether, if the devil helps me—' I did not finish the sentence.

"The bank was being put up to auction when I entered the salon. I secured it for two hundred louis. I had not reached the middle of my deal when I had already won two hundred and fifty thousand francs! But no longer would any of the players stake against me. *I was winning every game!*

"I was jubilant; I had never dreamt that such luck would be mine. I threw up the bank – i.e., what remained of it for me to hold. I next amused myself at throwing away chances, just to see what would happen. In spite of this I continued winning. Exclamations were heard on all sides. The players vowed I had the devil's own luck. I collected my winnings and left.

"No sooner had I reached the street when I began to think and to become alarmed. The coincidence between the scene of the wardrobe and of my extraordinary success as a banker troubled me. Of a sudden, and to my surprise, I found myself wending my way back to the club. I was resolved to probe the matter to the bottom. My short-lived joy was disturbed by the fact that I had not lost once. So it was that I was anxious to lose just once.

"When I left the club for the second time, at six o'clock in the morning, I had won, in money and on parole, no less than a couple of millions. But I had not once lost – not a single, solitary time. I felt myself becoming a raving madman. When I say that I had not lost once, I speak with regard to money, for when I had played for nothing, without stakes, to see, just for the fun of the matter, I lost inexorably. But no sooner had a punter staked even as low as half a franc against me, I won his money. It mattered little, a sou or a million francs. I could no longer lose. 'Thou shalt win!' Oh, that terrible curse! That curse! For a whole week did I try. I went into the worst gambling-hells. I sat down to card-tables presided over by card-sharpers; I won even from them; I won from one and all against whom I played. I did nothing but win!

"So, you no longer laugh, gentlemen! You scoff no more! You see now, good sirs, that one should never be in a hurry to laugh! I told you I had seen the devil! Do you believe me now? I possessed then the certainty, the palpable proof, visible to one and all, the natural and terrestrial proof of my revolting compact with the devil. The law of probabilities no longer existed as far as I was concerned. There were not even any probabilities. There remained only the supernatural certainty of winning eternally – until the day of death. Death! I could no longer dream of it as a desire. For the first time in my life I dreaded it. The terrors of death haunted me, because of what awaited me at the end!

"My uppermost thought was to redeem my soul – my wretched soul, my lost soul. I frequented the churches. I saw priests. I prostrated myself at the foot of the church steps. I beat my delirious head on the sacred flagstones! I prayed to God that I might lose, just as I had prayed to the devil that I might win. On leaving the holy place I was wont to hurry to some low gambling-den and stake a few louis on a card. But I continued winning for ever and ever! 'Thou shalt win!'

"Not for a single second did I entertain the idea of owing my happiness to those accursed millions. I offered up my heart to God as a burnt-offering, I distributed the millions I had won to the poor, and I came here, gentlemen, to await the death which spurns me – the death I dread!"

"You have never played since those days?" I asked.

"I have never played from that time until now."

Allan had read my thoughts. He too was dreaming that it might be possible to rescue from his monomania the man whom we both persisted in considering insane.

"I feel sure," he said, "that so great a sacrifice has won you pardon. Your despair has been undoubtedly sincere, and your punishment a terrible one. What more could Heaven require of you? In your place *I should try—*"

"You would try – what?" exclaimed the man, springing from his seat.

"I should try whether I were still doomed to win!"

The man struck the table a violent blow with his clenched fist.

"And so this is all the remedy you can suggest! So this is all the narrative of a curse transcending all things earthly has inspired you with? You seek to induce an old lunatic to play, with the object or demonstrating to him that he is not insane! For I read full well in your eyes what you think of me: 'He is mad, mad, mad!' You do not believe a single word of all I have told you. You think I am insane, young man! And you, too," he added, addressing Allan, "you think I am insane – mad, mad, mad! I tell you that I have seen the devil! Yes, your old madman has seen the devil! And he is going to prove it to you. The cards! Where are the cards?"

Espying them on the edge of the table, he sprang on them.

"It is you who have so willed it. I had harboured a supreme hope that I should die without having again made the infernal attempt, so that when my hour had come I might imagine that Heaven had forgiven me. Here are your cards! I will not touch them. They are yours. Shuffle them – deal me which you please – 'stack' them as you will. I tell you that I shall win. Do you believe me now?"

Allan had quietly picked up the cards.

The man, placing his hand on his shoulder, asked, "You do not believe me?"

"We shall see," replied Allan.

"What shall the stakes be?" I inquired.

"I do not know, gentlemen, whether you are well off or not, but I feel bound to inform you – you who have come to destroy my last hope – that you are ruined men."

Thereupon he took out his pocket-book and laid it on the table, saying:

"I will play you five straight points at écarté for the contents of this pocket-book. This just by way of a beginning. After that, I am willing to play you as many games as you see fit, until I cast you out of doors picked clean, your friends and yourself, ruined for the rest of your lives – yes, picked bare."

"Picked bare?" repeated Allan, who was far less moved than myself. "Do you want even our shirts?"

"Even your souls," cried the man, "which I intend to present to the devil in exchange for my own."

Allan winked at me, and asked:

"Shall we say 'Done,' and go halves in this?"

I agreed, shuffled the pack, and handed it to my

opponent.

He cut. I dealt. I turned up the knave of hearts. Our host looked at his hand and led. Clearly he ought not to have played the hand he held – three small clubs, the queen of diamonds, and the seven of spades. He took a trick with his queen, I took the four others, and, as he had led, I marked two points. I entertained not the slightest doubt that he was doing his utmost to lose.

It was his turn to deal. He turned up the king of spades. He could not restrain a shudder when he beheld that black-faced card, which, in spite of himself, gave him a trick.

He scanned his hand anxiously. It was my turn to call for cards. He refused them, evidently believing that he held a very poor hand; but my own was as bad as his, and he had a ten of hearts, which took my nine – I held the nine, eight, and seven of hearts.

He then played diamonds, to which I could not respond and two clubs higher than mine. Neither of us held a single trump. He scored a point, which, with the one secured to him by his king, gave him two. We were "evens," either of us being in a position to end matters at once if we made three points.

The deal was mine. I turned up the eight of diamonds. This time both of us called for cards. He asked for one, and showed me the one he had discarded – the seven of diamonds. He was anxious not to hold any trumps. His wish was gratified, and he succeeded in making me score another two points, which gave me four.

In spite of ourselves, Allan and I glanced towards the pocket-book. Our thoughts ran: "There lies a small fortune which is shortly to be ours, one which, in all conscience, we shall not have had much trouble in winning."

Our host dealt in his turn, and when I saw the cards he had given me I considered the matter as good as settled. This time he had not turned up a king, but the seven of clubs. I held two hearts and three trumps – the ace and king of hearts, the ace, ten, and nine of clubs. I led the king, my opponent followed with the queen; I flung the ace on the table, my opponent being compelled to take it with the knave of hearts, and he then played a diamond, which I trumped. I played the ace of trumps; he took it with the queen, but I was ready for him with my last card, the ten of clubs. He had the knave of trumps! As I had led he scored two, making "four all." Our host smothered a curse which was hovering on his lips.

"No need for you to worry," I remarked, "no one has won yet."

"We are about to prove to you," said Allan, in the midst of a deathly silence, "that you can lose just like any ordinary mortal."

Our host groaned, "I cannot lose."

The interest in the game was now at its height. A point on either side, and either of us would be the winner. If I turned up the king the game was ended, and I won twelve thousand francs from a man who claimed that he could not lose. I had dealt. I turned up the king – the king of hearts. I had won!

My opponent uttered a cry of joy. He bent over the card, picked it up, considered it attentively, fingered it, raised it to his eyes, and we thought that he was about to press it to his lips. He murmured:

"Great heavens, can it be? Then – then I have lost!"

"So it would seem," I remarked.

Allan added, "You now see full well that one should not place any faith in what the devil says."

The gentleman took his pocket-book and opened it.

"Gentlemen," he sighed, "bless you for having won all that is in this book. Would that it contained a million! I should gladly have handed it over to you."

With trembling hands he searched the pocket-book, emptying it of all its contents, with a look of surprise at not finding at once the twelve thousand francs he had deposited in its folds. They were not there!

The pocket-book, searched with feverish hands, lay empty on the table. *There was nothing in the pocket-book! Nothing*!

We sat dumbfounded at this inexplicable phenomenon –

the empty pocket-book! We picked it up and fingered it. We searched it carefully, only to find it empty. Our host, livid and as one possessed, was searching himself, and begging us to search him. We searched him – we searched him, because it was beyond our power to resist his delirious will; but we found nothing – nothing!

"Hark!" exclaimed our host. "Hark, hark! Does it not seem to you tonight that the wind sounds like the voice of a dog?"

We listened, and Makoko answered, "It is true! The wind really seems to be barking – there, behind the door!"

The door was shaking strangely, and we heard a voice calling, "Open!"

I drew the bolts and opened the door. A human form rushed into the room.

"It is the steward," I said.

"Sir, sir!" he ejaculated.

"What is it?" we all exclaimed, breathlessly, wondering what was about to follow.

"Sir, I thought I had handed you your twelve thousand francs. Indeed, I am positive I did so. Those gentlemen doubtless saw me."

"Yes, indeed," from all of us.

"Well, I have just discovered them in my bag. I cannot understand how it has happened. I have returned to bring them back to you – *once more.* Here they are."

The steward again pulled out the identical envelope, and a second time counted the twelve one-thousand-franc notes, adding:

"I know not what ails the mountainside tonight, but it terrifies me. I shall sleep here."

The twelve thousand francs were now lying on the table. Our host cried:

"This time we see them there, there before us! Where are the cards? Deal them. The twelve thousand in five straight points, to see, to know for certain. I tell you that I wish to know – *to know.*"

I dealt. My opponent called for cards; I refused them. He had five trumps. He scored two points. He dealt the cards. He turned up the king. I led. He again had five trumps. Three and two are five! He had won!

Then he howled; yes, howled like the wind which had the voice of a dog. He snatched the cards from the table and cast them into the flames. "Into the fire with the cards Let the fire consume them!" he shrieked.

Suddenly he strode towards the door. Outside a dog barked – a dog raising a death-howl.

The man reached the door, and speaking through it asked:

"Is that you, Mystère?"

To what phenomenon was it due that both wind and dog were silent simultaneously?

The man softly drew the bolts and half opened the door. No sooner was the door ajar than the infernal yelping broke out so prolonged and so lugubrious that it made us shiver to our very marrow. Our host had now flung himself upon the door with such force that we could almost think he had smashed it. Not content with having pushed back the bolts, he pressed with his knees and arms against the door, without uttering a sound. All we heard was his panting respiration.

Then, when the death-like yelping had ceased, and both within and without silence reigned supreme, the man, turning towards us and tottering forward, said:

"*He has returned! Beware!*"

Midnight. We have gone our respective ways. Makoko and Mathis have remained below beside the dying embers. Allan has sought his bedroom, while, driven by some unknown inner force controlling me absolutely, I find myself in the haunted room. I am repeating the doings of the man whose story we had heard that night; I select the same book, open it at the same page; I go to the same window; I pull the curtain aside; I gaze upon the same moonlit landscape, for the wind has long since driven off the tempest-clouds and the fog. I only see bare rocks, shining like steel under the rays of the bright moon, and – on the desolate plateau – a weirdly dancing shadow – the shadow of Mystère, with her formidable jaws wide apart – jaws that I can see barking. Do I hear the barking? Yes; it seems to me that I hear it. I let the curtain drop. I take my candlestick from the chest of drawers. I step towards the wardrobe. I look at myself in its mirrored panel. I dream of *him* who wrote the words which lie concealed within. Whose face is it that I see in the mirror? It is my own! But is it possible that the face of our host on the fatal night could have been more pallid than mine is now? In all truth, my face is that of a dead man. On one side – there – there – that little cloud – that misty cloudlet in the mirror – cheek by jowl with my face – those fearful eyes – those lips! Oh, if I could but scream! I cannot. I am powerless to cry out, *when suddenly I hear three knocks.* And – and my hand strays of its own accord towards the door of the wardrobe – my inquisitive hand – my accursed hand.

Of a sudden my hand is gripped in the vice I know so well. I look round. I am face to face with our host, who says to me in a voice which seems to come from another world:

"Do not open it!"

Epilogue

Next morning we did not ask our host to give us the opportunity of winning back our money. We fled from his roof without even taking leave of him. Twelve thousand francs were sent that evening to our strange host through Makoko's father, to whom we had told our adventure. He returned them to us, with the following note:

"We are quits. When we played, both the first game, which you won, and the second one, which you lost, we *believed*, you and I, that we were staking twelve thousand francs. That must be sufficient for us. The devil has my soul, but he shall not posses my honour."

We were not at all anxious to keep the twelve thousand francs, so we presented them to a hospital in La Chaux-de-Fonds which was in sore need of money. Following upon urgent repairs, to which our donation was applied, the hospital, one winter's night, was so thoroughly burned to the ground that at noon of the following day nothing but ashes remained of it.

www.ingramcontent.com/pod-product-compliance
Lightning Source LLC
Chambersburg PA
CBHW030534020726
47494CB00004B/1368